Heyward the Horse

Loves Charleston, Of Course!

Typeset in Hoefler Text and Gill Sans

First Printing, 2018
Printed in South Korea

ISBN 978-0-9997817-0-8

www.HeywardtheHorse.com

For Erin, Lucy and Sam.

Is it time to get up?
Is the sun in the sky?

I'm late and I can't find
my magic bow tie!

My name is
Heyward M. Pinckney the Fourth.

I'll give you a tour of
my city, of course!

Church bells are ringing
from steeples nearby.

That means we're late!
Where *is* my bow tie?

My work starts right here
in a stable downtown.

Hop up on board and
I'll show you around!

Waterfront Park –
the first stop on our ride.

Watch boats big and little,
all riding the tide.

Onward we go,
to your right...
Rainbow Row!

Historical houses
from long, long ago.

Remember the church bells we heard from before?

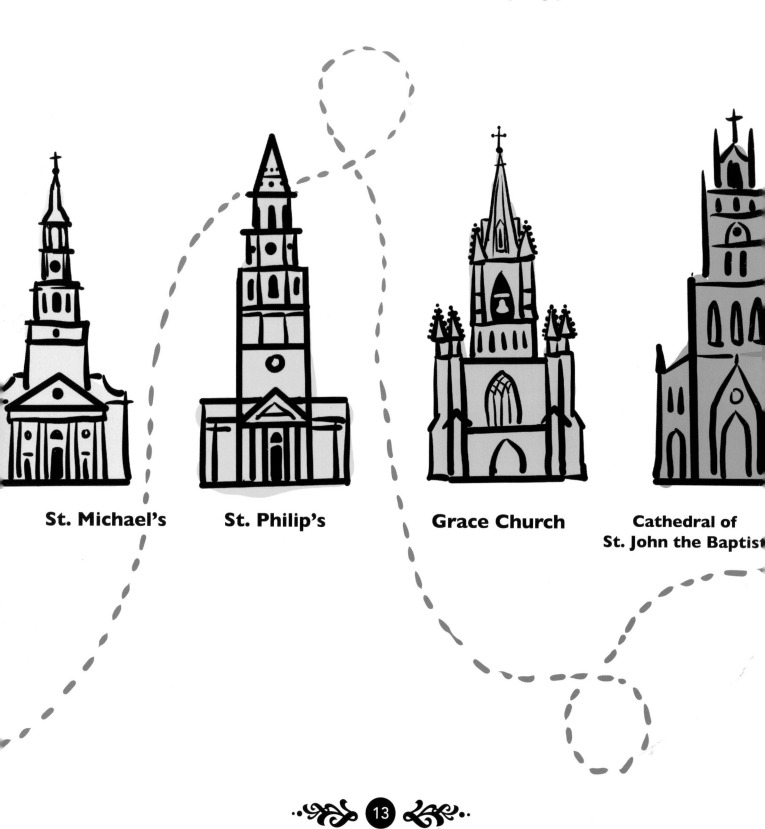

St. Michael's

St. Philip's

Grace Church

Cathedral of
St. John the Baptist

Here in our city, we have churches galore!

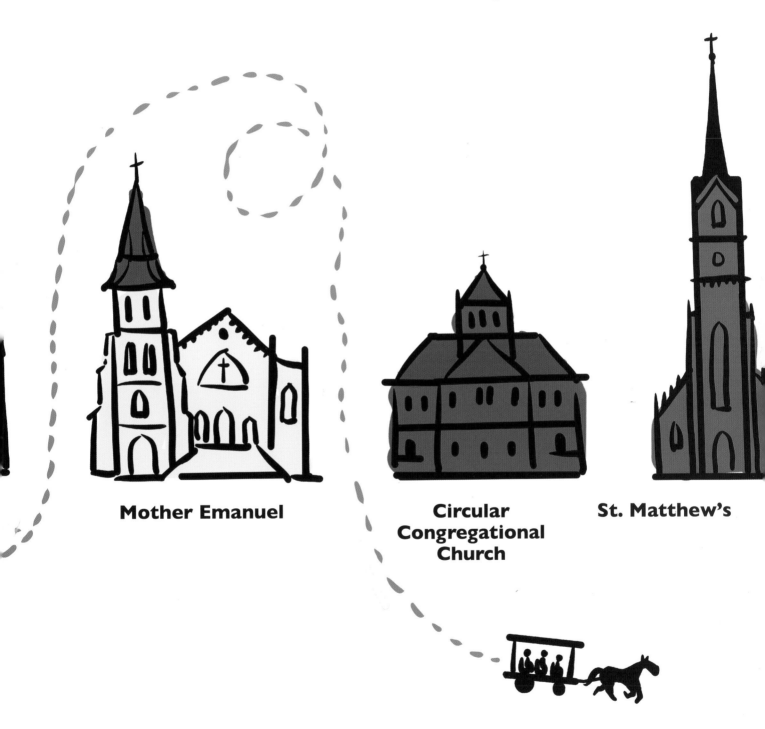

Mother Emanuel

Circular Congregational Church

St. Matthew's

Buy gifts at the market
from stalls that we pass.

May I suggest anything
made from sweetgrass.

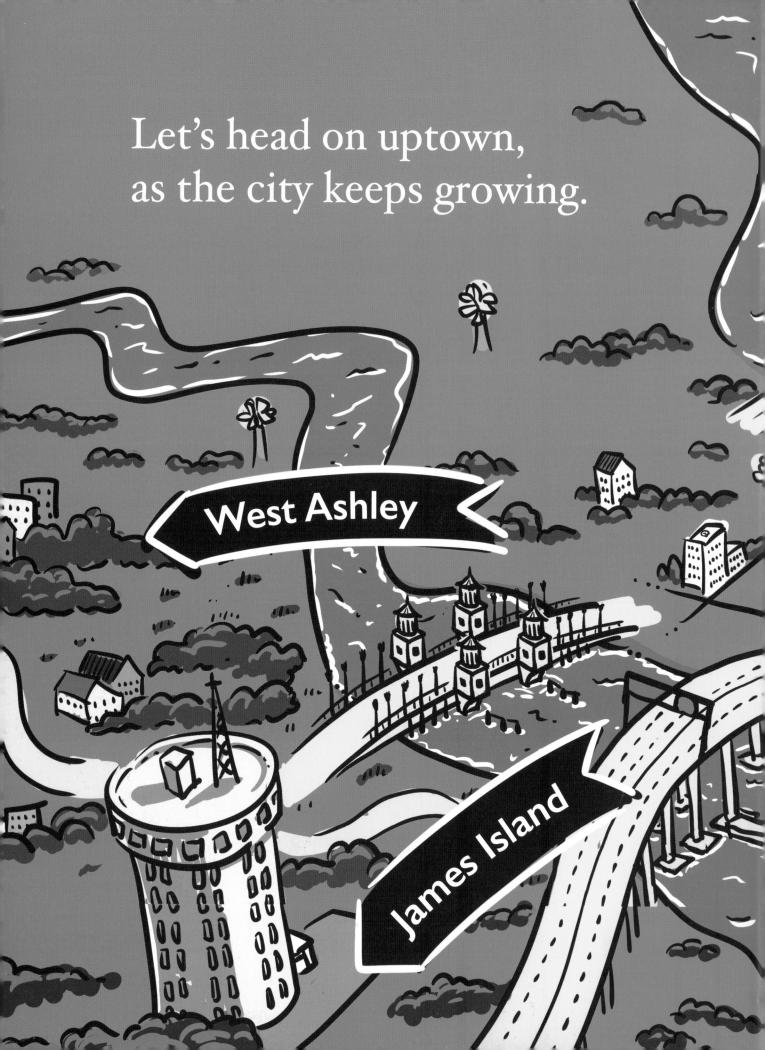

There are bridges all over
to places worth going.

Wait just a minute!
I see my bow tie!

It's magic, my darling,
and now...

WE
CAN
FLY!

Grab on to something
and hold on with care.

We'll check out the rest
of the city by air!

The town is surrounded
by marshes and pluff.

Smells kinda funny,
you get used to the stuff.

Angel Oak Tree

Morris Island Lighthouse

Drayton Hall

Take pictures of landmarks
that are just out of reach,

We'll end our grand tour
with sunset at the beach.

Oh, do come back soon
to see Heyward, ya hear?

For Charleston is lonely
without you, my dear!

About the Author and Illustrator

Andrew Barton is a designer, illustrator and children's book author in Charleston, S.C. He lives in West Ashley with his wife and two young children. He enjoys history, painting and the outdoors.

HeywardtheHorse.com